Puss in Palace

English version by Paul Sidey

Copyright © 1989 by Françoise and Frédéric Joos.
This special paperback edition first published in 2003 by Andersen Press Ltd.
The rights of Françoise and Frédéric Joos. to be identified as the author and illustrator of this work
have been asserted by them in accordance with the Copyright, Designs and Patents Act, 1988.
First published in Great Britain in 1989 by Andersen Press Ltd. 20 Vauxhall Bridge Road, London SW1V 2SA.
Published in Australia by Random House Australia Pty., 20 Alfred Street, Milsons Point, Sydney, NSW 2061.
All rights reserved. Colour separated in Switzerland by Photolitho AG, Zürich.
Printed and bound in China.

10 9 8 7 6 5 4 3 2 1

British Library Cataloguing in Publication Data available.

ISBN 1 84270 270 X

This book has been printed on acid-free paper

Puss in Palace

Françoise & Frédéric Joos

Andersen Press · London

Shall I tell you a strange and wonderful tale
Of a prince with whiskers and a tail?

A royal bath begins each day
And clockwork toys dive in to play.

His fur is brushed all smooth and nice
By faithful and adoring mice.

Sipping warm milk he starts to doze
While the artist paints a dashing pose.

He rarely walks upon four paws
Even when he's out of doors.

And reads the paper upside-down
As one small servant hauls him round.

He loves his daily serenade
But the tuneful trio's never paid.

Softly he snoozes, while a bunch
Of hungry mice take him to lunch.

One word of command and the food arrives.
How wonderful to have nine lives!

But a mouse's day is never done.
That pampered puss has all the fun.

In the palace pool it's bliss to float.
Why swim when you can take a boat?

He purrs with pleasure at puppet shows
When dogs get bonked upon the nose.

Jam sandwiches can taste quite yummy
Though twelve add up to a big fat tummy.

He's a master, he thinks, at the game of chess
And the mouse who wins is in a mess.

Which collar would look best today
On a plump young prince just off to play?

So little time, so much to see
And soon it will be time for tea.

A special game is tug-of-war
But the mice can't pull him to the floor.

He's not much good at catching flies
And hurls his slippers to the skies.

Rocked in a hammock all afternoon
He dreams of flying to the moon.

Those busy mice work day and night
To satisfy his appetite.

At night he tumbles into bed
And, tucked up, has a story read.

The toys know well the book will send
Their prince to sleep before the end.

The palace cat has a wonderful time.
Can you guess why? This cat is mine.